This storybook belongs to:

To my dear husband, Michael, and three sons, Michael Jr., Anthony and Justin ~ 3/84 ~

With special appreciation to:
Margo Lundell, editor
Stacie Rogoff, art director

When people from the village on the other side of the river tried to row over to Poppyseed Hill, the monster grew very angry. Gloo-Gloo, as he was called, thrashed his huge body in the water and made giant waves that splashed on the shore. Wind from his wild movements bent the trees by the river's edge.

Finally no one tried to cross the river anymore, and Miss Kessy gave up hoping for visitors.

Taragon was the bouncy little girl in pigtails who always tried hard to keep up with Poppyseed.

The red-haired girl with a round straw hat was named Cinamint for two good spices—cinnamon and mint.

The last child, a quiet little black girl, was named Mocha.

In the days that followed, Miss Kessy and the children lived happily together on Poppyseed Hill. Never did the children try to cross the river down below, for they remembered what Miss Kessy had told them—to stay away from the Gloo-Gloo Monster!

Mosky Mouse followed Poppyseed everywhere. When she went to pick apples, he scampered up the tree for her and dropped down the brightest red apples he could find.

All the children
found ways to help
Miss Kessy. Oregano
chopped kindling for
the stove.

Bayleave fetched
water at the pump.

The others helped
hang out the wash and
gather fresh flowers for
the table.

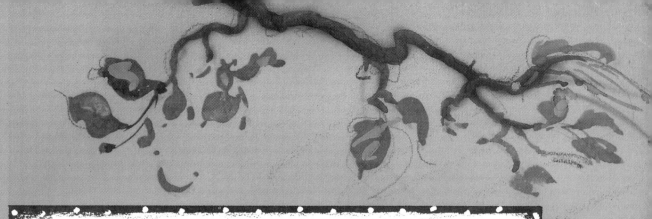

One day Poppyseed took freshly-baked cookies down the hill to the caretaker. While she was there, she saw children from the village playing on the other side of the river.

"If the monster didn't get angry," Poppyseed said to the caretaker, "we could cross the river and play with those children."

The caretaker, a wise old man with elf-like features, answered Poppyseed mysteriously, saying:

> *"Hear me well, and do not listen*
> *to the monster's angry song.*
> *Hear another deep within,*
> *deep within where songs belong."*

Poppyseed asked the caretaker to explain his words. When he would not, she walked slowly back up the hill. Inside the cottage she told Miss Kessy how very much she would like to play with the children on the riverbank.

Miss Kessy had an idea. If Poppyseed and the others couldn't play with the children across the river, at least they could send them cookies. The cookies could be carried across by the friendly white doves that lived on Poppyseed Hill.

The beautiful doves were happy to help Miss Kessy and the children. Fresh cookies were quickly wrapped in packages light enough for the birds to carry.

Soon one white dove after another was flying across the river. When the children on the other side received the little packages, they clapped their hands with delight.

Suddenly the waters in the river began to churn. A wind came up, and the sky darkened.

It was the angry monster—turning day into night.
Each time a dove crossed the river, the monster stirred
the waters more furiously. Waves crashed on the shore
and began to flood the caretaker's house.

The storm was so fierce that Miss Kessy and the children stopped sending the birds across the river. The doves returned to their roost. Little by little, the waters calmed, and the monster's tail disappeared from sight.

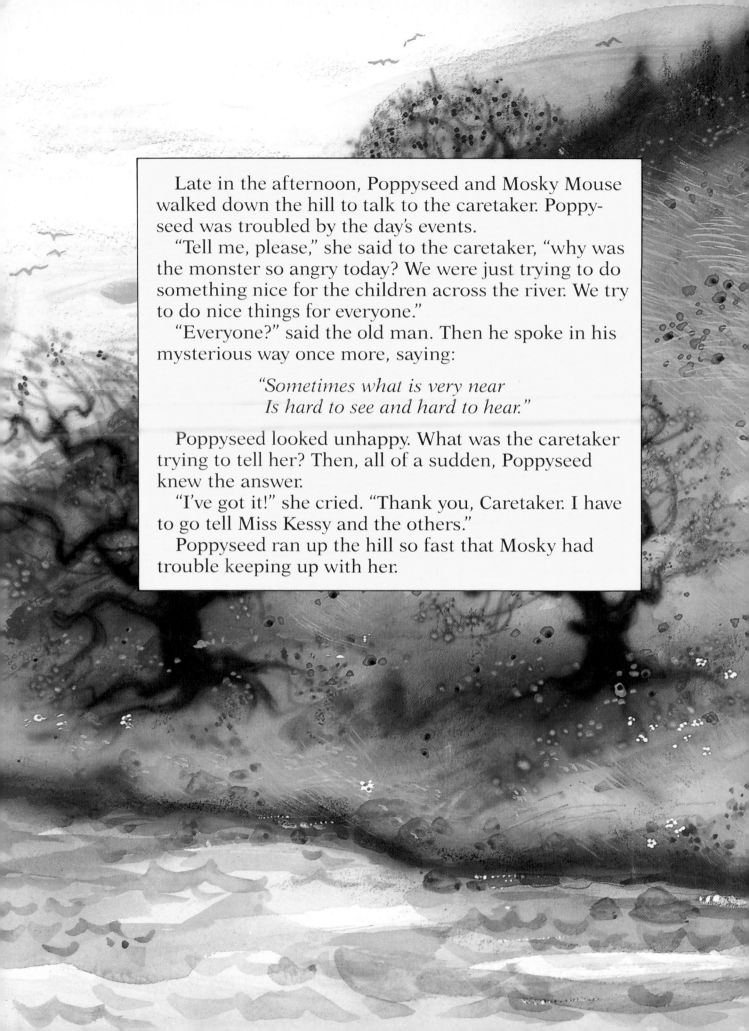

Late in the afternoon, Poppyseed and Mosky Mouse walked down the hill to talk to the caretaker. Poppyseed was troubled by the day's events.

"Tell me, please," she said to the caretaker, "why was the monster so angry today? We were just trying to do something nice for the children across the river. We try to do nice things for everyone."

"Everyone?" said the old man. Then he spoke in his mysterious way once more, saying:

"*Sometimes what is very near
Is hard to see and hard to hear.*"

Poppyseed looked unhappy. What was the caretaker trying to tell her? Then, all of a sudden, Poppyseed knew the answer.

"I've got it!" she cried. "Thank you, Caretaker. I have to go tell Miss Kessy and the others."

Poppyseed ran up the hill so fast that Mosky had trouble keeping up with her.

She burst into the cottage where Miss Kessy was reading to the children.

"Excuse me, Miss Kessy," she said, "but I've just figured out why the monster gets so mad when we go near the river. It's because we don't pay any attention to him. We haven't tried to be his friend."

Miss Kessy thought Poppyseed just might be right. She suggested that they bake a monster-sized cookie the very next day and offer it to Gloo-Gloo as a present.

Right after breakfast the next morning, the children gathered around to help Miss Kessy mix a very large batch of cookie dough. A cookbook lay nearby, unopened. Miss Kessy knew the recipe by heart.

She explained to the children that they would bake the cookie in sections, then glue the sections together with icing. The monster's cookie would have to be big—nearly as big as the kitchen table!

While the others worked, Mosky Mouse made up a little baking song:

"Mix and measure,
stir and bake.
Not a pie.
Not a cake.

Just one cookie
full of spice.
Miss Kessy's cookie
will be nice!"

When the cookie was nearly finished, Poppyseed wrote a poem for the monster. She did not know if Gloo-Gloo could read, but she wanted to give it to him just in case he could.

Gloo-Gloo Monster,
it is true,
this great big cookie's
just for you.
We will bring you
flowers, too.
Please be our friend,
oh please, Gloo-Gloo.

love,
Poppyseed.

Then Poppyseed, Taragon, and Mosky went down the poppy-covered hillside and began to weave a crown of crimson flowers for the monster.

Taragon was excited and danced across the field as she gathered flowers. Mosky, however, was nervous about meeting the monster. "We don't know how big he is," said the little mouse. "How shall we know what size to make his crown?"

"Don't worry about the size, Mosky," said Poppyseed. "The important thing is, will Gloo-Gloo accept our presents at all?"

By the time the children started down to the river with their gifts, it was late afternoon. All of them were a little afraid of meeting the monster. Miss Kessy came along to give the children courage.

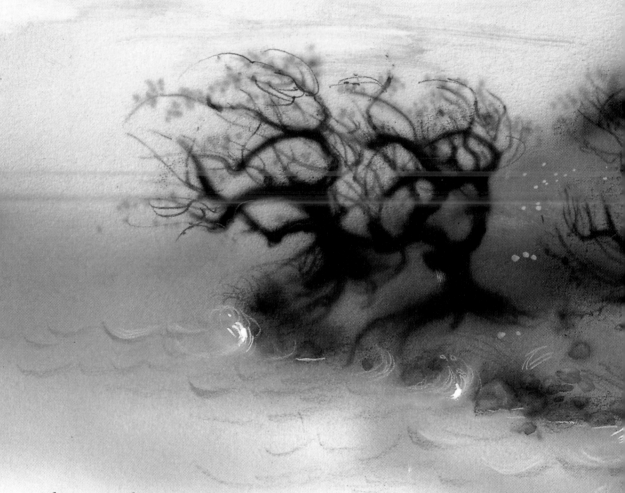

The caretaker met Poppyseed at the bottom of the hill. They looked out at the river, but the monster was nowhere to be seen. Poppyseed began to hope that they wouldn't see the monster after all.

The old caretaker tried to encourage her. "Don't be afraid," he said. "Just call out his name—the way you would call to a friend."

Poppyseed walked nearer to the water's edge.

"Gloo-Gloo," she called. "Where are you? We have presents for you."

The other children reached the bottom of the hill, and
they, too, began to call: "Gloo-Gloo, where are you?"

Then Poppyseed and Oregano saw dark whirlpools in the flowing river. That meant the monster was there and had heard them calling.

Oregano spotted a round bump in the water. It was the top of the monster's head!

Suddenly the monster rose quietly from the water.
Gloo-Gloo was huge! Poppyseed's heart beat very fast.
Oregano looked pale and began pulling back from the
river's edge.

"Oregano, we mustn't run away!" whispered
Poppyseed, even though she, too, was very frightened.
"Quick, give him the cookie!"

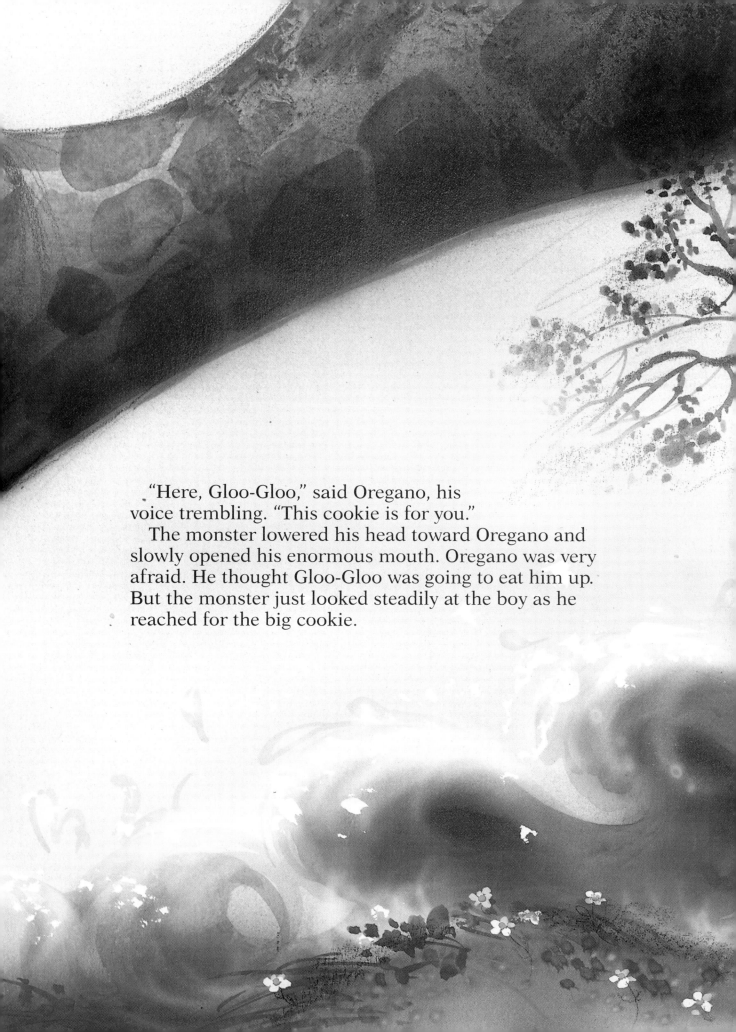

"Here, Gloo-Gloo," said Oregano, his voice trembling. "This cookie is for you."

The monster lowered his head toward Oregano and slowly opened his enormous mouth. Oregano was very afraid. He thought Gloo-Gloo was going to eat him up. But the monster just looked steadily at the boy as he reached for the big cookie.

Not only did Gloo-Gloo like his cookie, but he also let Poppyseed put the crown of flowers on his head. He even smiled when she read him her poem. Then he gestured to all the children as if inviting them onto his back.

Miss Kessy couldn't believe her eyes. The monster wasn't a monster at all. He was altogether friendly! Miss Kessy stood onshore with the caretaker while Gloo-Gloo gently carried the children across the river. At last they could visit the children on the other side.

Never again were Poppyseed and the others afraid of the monster. And the children in the village also learned to trust Gloo-Gloo. Whenever they wanted to visit Poppyseed, he ferried them across the river as smoothly as he was able.

The days that followed were busy and happy. There were cookies to bake for Gloo-Gloo and hugs and kisses to give to Miss Kessy. In the evenings, Bayleave played his violin while the sun sank slowly down.

The song that Bayleave played was a song to say thank you—for a snug cottage on a gentle slope, a home on Poppyseed Hill.

Spend your days with a happy heart !!!